CIRCUS OF THE WOLVES

**For my son Zachary —
I love you**
—JB

To Albert and Marian Hubbell
—RAP

LOTHROP, LEE & SHEPARD BOOKS
NEW YORK

Text copyright © 1994 by Jack Bushnell
Illustrations copyright © 1994 by Robert Andrew Parker

First Edition 1 2 3 4 5 6 7 8 9 10

Library of Congress Cataloging in Publication
Bushnell, Jack. Circus of the wolves / by Jack Bushnell; illustrated by Robert Andrew Parker.
  p.   cm.   Summary: Kael, a black timber wolf, is captured and performs for a circus, until he has the opportunity to escape. ISBN 0-688-12554-9.—ISBN 0-688-12555-7 (lib. bdg.) 1. Circus—Fiction. [1. Wolves—Fiction.] I. Parker, Robert Andrew, ill. II. Title. PZ7.B96547C1 1994
[Fic]—dc20 93-8092 CIP AC

JACK BUSHNELL

CIRCUS OF THE WOLVES

ROBERT ANDREW PARKER

Kael, a black timber wolf with eyes like light, joined the Summerson-Appleby Circus quite by accident. One moment, he was chasing a hare along the dawn shore of Lake Superior, scattering October leaves like startled butterflies. The next, the earth opened beneath him, tumbling him headlong into a deep pit.

Though he wasn't hurt, the damp and dark at the bottom of the hole frightened Kael. He spent a long day trying to escape, but the pit's walls were too high. He spent a long night crying for his mate and for his two pups waiting far away in the den.

In the morning, three men came with a net. They fired a sleeping dart into his hip. And when he awoke, he had joined the circus.

On his very first day, he was visited by a tall man with blue eyes and golden hair. "I have never seen a wolf so beautiful as you," the man told him softly. "You are the color of rich shale and the size of one of our small ponies. But your eyes…" The man leaned forward, and his golden hair fell loosely about his ears. "Your eyes are like fire."

Growls rumbled deep in Kael's chest, and the fur stood up on his shoulders. Twice he lunged at his cage bars, unable to reach the man outside them.

"They brought you to me," the man said, "because they know of my love for wolves." His voice sounded kind, but also strong. He smelled like green wood in winter, sweet and crisp, but with a hint of something bitter, not from the forest. "We will be good to you here," he said. "I hope you will even be happy with us."

But Kael was not happy. He paced all day, snarling and snapping if someone came too close. He wanted to leap through the bars and send all these people running like a herd of whitetail deer.

That night, the wolf raised his voice in a wail of sorrow and aloneness, the kind of aloneness that drifts down at twilight from the peak of a bald mountain and settles into the dark, still surface of a lake. He howled for his lost family, for jack pine forests in the deep snow of winter, for open grass-lands under a warm white moon.

In the darkness, the man came to him. "You are afraid I will take your soul from you," he whis-pered through the bars. "Don't be afraid, for I would never do that. Without your soul, you would not be beautiful or wonderful. And without beauty or wonder, there would be no circus."

All night, Kael growled and whimpered and panted as he paced back and forth. All night, the man sat near the cage, but not too near, talking softly to the wolf.

Finally, the sun rose above the trees. On the other side of his cage, eyes glinting in the early light, Kael listened to the sounds the man made when he spoke, the rustling of *s*'s, the insect whirr of *r*'s and *n*'s, the gentle pop of parting lips. While the circus awoke around them, Kael stared unblinking at the man with the golden hair.

From then on, the man visited the wolf several times each day, and he talked softly, but firmly, about all sorts of things. Though Kael did not, of course, know what the words meant, he heard the gentle strength in the man's voice.

Other wolves had come before Kael. They watched quietly as he prowled his cage. They looked into his yellow eyes with their own. While his glared with the brilliance of the sun, theirs reflected only the dark bars surrounding them. They smelled like wolves and looked like wolves, but something about them confused Kael and made him avoid their gaze.

But there was much more than other wolves for Kael to see and hear. Sullen tigers rippling orange and black. Bicycle-riding bears. Roaring, growling lions. Elephants with ears like giant leaves. During the day, the circus performers practiced their acts outdoors. Men and women in glittering costumes ran, leapt, tumbled, walked high above the ground on the thinnest of wires. As he watched, Kael paced his cage. In the evenings, circus children played loudly at tag, hid behind trailers, dashed screaming in and out among clothes hanging on lines to dry. The noises made Kael's quiet forest seem far away.

And such smells! The scent of cotton candy, so sweet and thick that he licked his lips trying to taste it in the air. The heavy, sharp odor of all those animals brought together in one place. The slightly sour, restless smell of people.

All these things filled Kael's ears, his eyes, and his nostrils each day, but they did not fill his nights. In his dreams, he dozed on a sunny hillside near his den, his belly full from the hunt, or splashed in a summer pond, or ran with his mate along a rocky ridge in spring. He dreamed of plowing through deep snow, his chest aching with the cold, his nostrils open for the scent of rabbit or deer. Winter was the hardest time for a wolf, but Kael loved the clarity of its crystal air and the stillness of snow.

As the weeks passed and the circus traveled south for the winter, Kael spent more and more time with the man. He grew to tolerate his visits and eventually came to look forward to them. The man's voice, rising and falling with the gentle insistence of a forest stream, soothed the wolf. And his eyes, blue, unblinking, direct, were so honest in their intensity that Kael could not help but trust them.

The day came when the wolf allowed the man to reach between the bars and touch his fur. Some time after that, he let him fasten a collar around his neck, though he scratched at it for days trying to knock it loose. And eventually he joined the man on walks. He could feel the man's strength through the leash at his neck, even as he strained to be free.

On their first visit to the big tent, they stood at the center of the ring, the man holding the rope tied to Kael's collar, his hand resting lightly against the wolf's warm fur. "This is a kind of charmed place," Kael heard the man say. "Almost everything in the circus happens in this circle...or above it." The wolf looked up toward the canvas roof, lit through by a bright sun. "Outside the ring are the crowds who come to watch. People of all sizes, with different smells and voices. People who laugh and who become afraid. You'll see."

What Kael saw that day were empty bleachers, dangling ropes, large hanging spotlights. He smelled the man. He smelled the musky odor of canvas. He smelled the harsh tang of sweat trapped over the years in the rough wood of rows and rows of seats. And he listened to the soft power of the man's voice.

"Here it's as if you are surrounded by a window, but a window of light and air. The trick is to reach through that window to all those people, and pull them toward you without breaking it." The man's eyes were bright as he looked at Kael. "You must never leave the ring. You can never bring them inside it. But you must make them feel as if you have."

With the man's help over many weeks, Kael learned to run the circle at a steady, loping pace, to clear hurdles without breaking stride, to jump straight into the air and catch a brightly colored ring in his teeth.

He learned by watching, for everything that Kael did, they did together. The man coaxed him, nudged him, ran with him, leapt with him, hugged him, and laughed with delight each time Kael learned something new.

The life of the circus was gradually becoming Kael's life. The sounds he heard were circus sounds. The sights he saw were circus sights. The air he breathed was circus air. In the midst of all this, the man's voice calmed the wolf. In that voice, Kael heard the whisper of water from a spring, the soothing creak of tall trees on a windy day. He felt the presence of something quiet and strong and lasting.

But he never felt the man's power more than when they were howling. At first they practiced alone in the big tent, the man raising his chin and calling to the roof. The man started low, but abruptly his voice rose clear and loud. Then, from a height, it descended and faded into silence. Kael had howled like that his whole life, before the hunt, before sleep, but he had never before heard a human being make that sound.

He soon understood that the man expected him to howl too. Slowly, slowly, Kael imitated the man who was imitating a wolf.

At first his howls were short, more like loud yawns, and he made them only in response to the man's noises. But it was not long before the wolf forgot the man in the midst of his song.

The howl is a wolf's music, and Kael's floated up and out of the ring, filling the huge tent with crystal notes. The song took him far away. He sang of the forests and valleys where he had hunted for food, of the icy pleasure of winter's first snowfall. He sang of the deer, and his body trembled with the joy and ache of the hunting call. And as he sang, the canvas of the tent seemed to tremble with him.

Over the next few weeks, the man brought other wolves to the ring, one at a time, to join Kael. When they could stand together without growling or fighting, the man began to teach them all to sing. At first they didn't understand what he wanted them to do. But after a time, Kael's voice prompted the others to raise their voices with him in a ghostly chorus that made five wolves sound as if they were fifty.

These wolves were not like any Kael remembered from the forest, not so curious, not so playful. But when they howled together, he forgot their strangeness. Then, for a short while, they became like him.

On the night of Kael's first performance, a humid April night in Monroe, Louisiana, the man placed the howl at the end of the program. The small crowd had been restless all evening, but when the man raised his arm and the lights in the tent dimmed almost to darkness, the crowd grew still.

When he lowered his arm, the wolves began.

It was disjointed at first. There were yips and barks and loud whines, like heavy drops of rain before a thunderstorm. But soon the wolves found their voices and the torrent swept out over the audience. Full-throated, loud and hollow, as if it came from the deep black sky, the chorus rose and fell. In the near-darkness, children moved closer to their parents, and adults felt their hearts beat faster. Drenched by sound, they were caught in the rush of mountain night music, a downhill rush that deepened and grew grander with each note. The beauty and power of it made them forget where they were until, as the music gradually softened, they felt as if a cold slow river was tugging them away.

Afterward, Kael knew that he too had been carried away by the song. He felt stronger, freer, than he had felt since the day he joined the circus. As the audience rose in joyous applause, he looked at the man and his heart was glad.

In the months that followed, the wolves always closed the evening's performance. From one town to the next, the crowds grew larger. The Summerson-Appleby Circus became known in the south, and then in the midwest, as the Circus of the Wolves. Even in bad weather, the bleachers were full.

Spring had passed, and summer was well along, when the circus headed north again through Mississippi, Arkansas, and Missouri. The man visited his newest performer every evening and talked to the wolf until the sun had set. Sometimes he even thanked Kael.

"Did you know," he asked, "that before you came, my wolves would not howl? They were all born in the circus, and they're wonderful performers. But I could not inspire them to sing." As always, Kael listened and felt soothed by the sounds of the man's voice. "They had begun to perform without pleasure, I think. And then you came. You brought life to them again."

The man with the golden hair reached between the cage bars and buried his fingers in warm wolf fur. Together they listened to the night, to crickets and frogs and the bark of a dog across a freshly mown field.

But in the days that followed, Kael became nervous. He didn't know why. His cage felt small. He paced, as if constant motion would stretch it larger.

Each new journey from one town to another, each mile farther north along dark straight highways, confused him more and more. When he was howling, when he shared the ring with the man and the other wolves, Kael knew only that. But alone in his cage, his nose to the breeze, he began to remember things. Tawny fur. The white flag of a tail. Slender, powerful legs that could outdistance him in a moment if he hesitated.

Then one night Kael smelled a new smell. The scent of wolf. Not circus wolves, but one out there, in the darkness, hunting. Kael stood utterly still in his cage, opened his nostrils, sensed unhurried movement through the trees. But he did not call to the other wolf. He sat in silence until morning.

Shortly after sunrise, the man arrived.

"We are near your home," he told Kael, reaching through the bars to stroke the wolf's fur. "You feel it, don't you?" They both looked into the distance, where the orange dawn cast a haze over the forests. "I'm sorry," the man said. "I know you must miss it."

Two days later, when the trucks stopped in the early morning, Kael sniffed the breezes that blew from a stand of spruce not far away. Quite suddenly he knew that he had been in those woods. He knew he had rested on the hill just visible beyond them. He knew one more thing, and it made his chest ache with longing and fear. His den and his family were out there.

That night it happened. After the performance had ended and the visitors had all left, one of the boys arrived with Kael's dinner and opened the cage door to place it inside. Suddenly loud smashing noises came from one of the pens, then the shrill trumpeting of a frightened elephant. No one ever knew for sure what the trouble was, though some later thought a raccoon had gotten in, looking for food. People came running from all over the circus. The boy was curious too, and when he ran toward the elephant pen, he forgot to close the wolf's cage door.

At first Kael did not know what to do. He had never left his cage before without a leash tied to his neck. His heart pounding, he stepped outside. He filled his nostrils with the smells of pine and new leaves, rabbits and deer.

Then he heard the man's voice. "I was afraid this might happen," the man said. They were alone, facing each other in the darkness, many yards apart. "I know this is hard for you," he added. Then he smiled. "After all, you were not born to be a circus wolf." At that moment, other men appeared with ropes and nets to capture Kael. The man with the golden hair waved them away.

"I saw their faces tonight," he whispered when they were alone again. He did not take his eyes from the wolf. "They trembled when you bared your teeth. They could not breathe when you howled. You bring to them a beauty and a power they can find nowhere else in their lives. You amaze them and delight them."

The sounds of the words beckoned Kael. But he heard other voices now. Night voices. Rustling, squeaking, hooting. Calling to him from the blackness beyond the circus. Kael knew he could not go to the man, and in that moment he stepped away.

"If you leave, you take beauty and power from those people." The man lowered his head and was silent. When he looked at Kael again, there were tears in his eyes. He sighed. "You were not born to be a circus wolf," he repeated. "But you are the greatest I have ever seen."

The man looked at the wall of trees in the distance. He took a deep breath, his nose in the air. To Kael, he looked like a wolf testing the wind.

"Go," he said. His cheeks were wet, but he smiled at Kael. "Go. If I were you, I would do the same."

Later that night, from far away, Kael would howl one more time for the man. But now he turned and walked toward the forest. He picked up scents of small animals, and he heard movements deep among the trees. The darkness began to close around him.

Once he stopped and looked back. The man stood where he had left him. Behind him, in the cages, were the silhouettes of the other wolves. The man raised his hand. "Good-bye," he called.

In the next moment, Kael had plunged into the woods, branches brushing against his fur, pine needles shifting beneath his paws.

By morning, with luck, he would be with his family again.

By morning, he would be a wolf again.

A NOTE FROM THE AUTHOR

I'VE NEVER HEARD OF A WOLF PERFORMING IN A CIRCUS, which is largely why I created that very thing in this book. It began years ago as a story to my young son, Zachary. At that time, I told of a tiger brought from the jungle. But when I sat down to write it, I decided I wanted a less familiar animal, an animal mysterious and powerful enough to embody a natural world as distinct and separate from the human world as possible. I wanted an animal that could be trained, but that would never really lose its aloofness and its wild need to be free. A wolf seemed perfect.

Many captive wolves can and do come to trust the human beings who look after them. Just as they are playful in the wild, some wolves in captivity become playful and even affectionate with their caretakers, like big rough dogs that don't know their own strength. But the process of building trust takes time, and it is here that I have taken some liberties. I have shortened the period during which the wolf undergoes his training so that the story can unfold in the span of a single year, one complete circuit through the American midwest and midsouth of my fictional circus. In reality, the process would take longer. Wild wolves try instinctively to stay clear of people and, because individual wolves have their own personalities, many never adapt to life in captivity.